Winnie-the-Pooh

The Big Adventure

A lift-the-flap book

EGMONT

Meet
Winnie-the-Pooh
and his friends.

When Christopher Robin woke up he knew at once that it was a day for **big boots** and **Adventure.** He studied his map. "Adventure can be tricky to find," he said to himself. "I shall need some help from Pooh."

Mr SANDERS

RING ALSO

Where's Pooh?

"I think," said Winnie-the-Pooh, solemnly,
"that it's easier to find things after a little smackerel."
He took a small lick of honey, and then a **bigger** one
for luck, and was ready to go.

They went to call on Piglet.

"He is a Very Small Animal," said Pooh.
"But if the Adventure is hiding close
to the ground he'll be sure to find it."

Soon they came to a gloomy part of the forest
and there Eeyore, Tigger, Kanga, Roo and Rabbit
all joined in with the hunt.

"Owww,"
said Winnie-the-Pooh,
finding something that was close
to the ground but **NOT** an adventure.

Can you find
Rabbit?

It wasn't long before they came to a stream.
They **wibbled** and **wobbled** over the stones and
Owl flew above them offering helpful advice like,
"Watch out for the water,"
until they were all
safely across.

How many
stepping stones
are there?

It was then
that they found the
Adventure . . .

It was green . . .
and it shook . . . and it swayed . . .
and it groaned . . . and it grumbled.
"A Woozle," squealed a terribly-frightened
Little Piglet. "Or is it a Wizzle?"

The sun was low in the trees
as the friends trooped, sleepily,
back to their homes and off to bed.

That night their dreams were
full of **Friendly Adventure** . . .

. . . and **cakes** with
cherries on the top.

Say goodnight to Pooh.

EGMONT
We bring stories to life

First published in Great Britain 2018 by Egmont UK Limited
The Yellow Building, 1 Nicholas Road, London, W11 4AN
www.egmont.co.uk

Written by Jane Riordan
Designed by Katie Bennett, Pritty Ramjee and Jillian Williams
Illustrations by Angela Rozelaar, Eleanor Taylor and Mikki Butterley

Based on the 'Winnie-the-Pooh' works by
A.A.Milne and E.H.Shepard
Copyright © Disney Enterprises Inc. 2018

ISBN 978 1 4052 9107 1
59865/1
Printed in China